Rigatoni the Pasta Cat

MICHAEL ROSEN

ILLUSTRATED BY TONY ROSS

Andersen Press

Please do not feed your cat pasta.
It's only for cats in stories.

First published in 2022 by
Andersen Press Limited
20 Vauxhall Bridge Road, London, SW1V 2SA, UK
Vijverlaan 48, 3062 HL Rotterdam, Nederland
www.andersenpress.co.uk

2 4 6 8 10 9 7 5 3 1

The rights of Michael Rosen and Tony Ross to be identified as the author and
illustrator of this work have been asserted by them in accordance with
the Copyright, Designs and Patents Act, 1988.

Text copyright © Michael Rosen, 2022
Illustrations copyright © Tony Ross, 2022

British Library Cataloguing in Publication Data available.

ISBN 978 1 78344 843 2

Printed and bound in Great Britain by Clays Ltd, Elcograf S.p.A.

Chapter One

Rigatoni loved pasta.

Rigatoni was a cat.

Rigatoni was a cat who loved pasta.

He loved **spaghetti**.

He loved penne.

He loved fusilli.

He loved linguini.

He loved ziti.

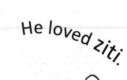

He loved vermicelli.

Rigatoni loved pasta.

He loved any kind of pasta no matter how it was served up:

with pesto

in soup

in lasagne

in cannelloni

with tomato sauce

any whichever way he got it.

Rigatoni was very lucky.

He was looked after by Ruth and Tina. They made sure that Rigatoni got some spaghetti, penne, fusilli, linguini, ziti or vermicelli every day. At least once every day.

If by some tiny chance, come five o'clock Ruth or Tina hadn't remembered Rigatoni's pasta, Rigatoni had a special pasta miaow to remind them. It was longer and deeper, as if he was saying,

"Pastaaaaaaaa!"

And when Rigatoni said,

"Pastaaaaaa!"

either Ruth or Tina jumped to it and

quickly put some pasta on the stove.

Then, when they dished it up in Rigatoni's special pasta dish, they would listen to Rigatoni making noises that meant he was loving it:

"Mmmmmm, pastaaaa . . . mmmm . . . prrrrr."

This is how it was.

Day after day in Rigatoni's home.

And his favourite place on the cushion on the sofa.

Until . . . until . . .
Until, what?
Until, one day Ruth and
Tina had to go away.

Oh no!

Chapter Two

Yes, Ruth and Tina had to go away to another town because Ruth's mother wasn't very well.

Rigatoni didn't know this until he started seeing Ruth and Tina tidying up, putting things into suitcases and bags, and making long phone calls.

And then, in the middle of all this busyness, they brought over George.

"This is George," Tina said. "We're not taking you with us, Rigatoni, but you'll be all right because George is going to come in every day, give you your food and stroke you."

Rigatoni looked at George. He went over to his leg and smelled him. It smelled of some kind of scent that Rigatoni had noticed that boys like putting on. But Rigatoni didn't like it.

Rigatoni looked up at George hoping for a stroke, or a tickle. George did just that. He bent down, gave Rigatoni a nice stroke and then a good old tickle underneath his chin. Rigatoni purred.

"He likes that," said Tina. "A bit of that every day will be just right."

Then, a day later, Ruth and Tina left.

Rigatoni watched them leave. He wondered when they would be back. No way of knowing. It made him sad to see them walking off with the suitcases and bags, packing them into the back of the car and then the car moving off down the street.

I wonder when George will be over, Rigatoni thought. *I'm getting hungry.*

I'm getting hungry for my pasta.

Chapter Three

He didn't have to wait long. Rigatoni heard the key turning in the lock and there was George.

Rigatoni pattered up to George and pushed himself against George's leg, even though it still smelled of that scent.

"Yes, yes, yes," said George, just a little bit snappily. "Keep your hair on, mate. I've got your breakfast."

George took a tin of "Good Mews" cat food out of his pocket, opened it up and forked it into Rigatoni's bowl.

Rigatoni looked at it. It wasn't that he didn't like Good Mews. And he certainly didn't hate it. But he didn't *really* like it. And he most certainly didn't *love* it.

George bent down, gave Rigatoni a stroke, and waited while Rigatoni made his mind up whether to eat his bowlful of Good Mews or not.

But Rigatoni wasn't sure.

He went on sniffing it, starting to eat it, stopping, giving it a lick, then stopping.

George gave him another stroke.

Oh well, Rigatoni thought, *I'll give it a go*, and he put his face right in close to the pile of Good Mews in his bowl and started to chew it.

It was OK. It wasn't awful. Rigatoni munched away. And once Rigatoni got stuck in to it, George stood up, called out, "Bye, mate! See you later."

Oh, thought Rigatoni, *I didn't get a tickle, did I?*

But really, he was thinking something else. He was thinking, *What about pasta? Is this George boy going to give me pasta when he comes back?*

He went to lie down on the cushion on the sofa, but then changed his mind and pushed the cat flap in the back door and went outside to have a lie down in the sun instead.

The day passed.

A squirrel came very close, sat up on its back legs, nibbled at something, made a sort of "chirrup" noise and scampered off.

Rigatoni moved on to his other side and fell asleep again.

Chapter Four

When Rigatoni woke up, he was hungry.

He went back to the cat flap, gave it a push and strolled round the flat.

He could still smell Ruth and Tina where they liked to sit. But they weren't there, were they?

I wonder when they'll be back, he thought. *And I wonder if they miss me? Are they thinking, "Oh, if only Rigatoni was with us?"*

Then he heard the key in the lock and it was George again.

Rigatoni rushed up to George and pushed against his leg. "Yes, yes, yes," said George, "I'm here, don't worry."

And again, he took out of his pocket a tin of Good Mews.

Rigatoni looked at it. *Oh no*, he thought, *it's Good Mews again. He's not going to make me any pasta.*

And sure enough, George forked out the Good Mews into Rigatoni's pasta bowl.

It was so disappointing.
So dull.
So sad.

George watched him.

"Go on then, mate," George said. "It's Good Mews. You like that, don't you?" George leaned down and gave Rigatoni a bit of a stroke.

But it didn't help. Rigatoni missed pasta. He missed spaghetti, penne, fusilli, linguini, ziti and vermicelli, whichever way it came, lasagne or cannelloni. He missed it so much, it felt like there was a great big hole in his belly and nothing could fill it: not Good Mews, nothing. The only thing that could fill it was a lovely big bowlful of pasta.

But it wasn't there.
Just a pile of Good Mews.

George waited for a while but when he saw that Rigatoni wasn't going to eat any, he just shrugged, muttering something to himself about how he thought Rigatoni would get round to it later. And then off he went.

Rigatoni started to worry. *Is this how it's going to be?*

All George is going to give me is Good Mews?

Day after day?

And . . . He could hardly bear to say it to himself, *And* . . . *no pasta?!*

Just thinking "no pasta" made him shudder. How could he live without pasta?

After a bit, in this state of worry and sadness, Rigatoni wandered round and round his pasta bowl, making up his mind whether to eat the Good Mews.

In the end he sniffed it, licked it and gave it a bit of chew. It wasn't horrible. It wasn't revolting. It was just about OK. *Yes,*

yes,

yes, he said to himself, thinking of George, *but it's not PASTA!*

He chewed his way through most of it but really couldn't bring himself to eat all of it. He couldn't bring himself to lick the bowl clean like he did with PASTA!

Oh imagine if this had been a lovely big bowl of spaghetti and pesto . . .

or a beautiful bowlful of cannelloni . . .

or a lovely pile of whirly fusilli he could bury his whiskers in . . .

oh if only,

if only,

if only.

But there was nothing he could do.

Chapter Five

And it was the same story the next day.

George. Good Mews. Out through the back door for a sleep. Watch the squirrel scampering about and chewing on something.

Then back indoors and George again. Good Mews again.

Just that.

Then a big thought came to Rigatoni.

What if Ruth and Tina are away for ages? For ages and ages?

But then came another even bigger thought.

What if Ruth and Tina never come back?

Never, *ever*, *ever*.

And all he had from now and for ever was Good Mews?

No more pasta. Ever again.

Oh nooooo!

Rigatoni felt horror at the thought of it. It felt terrible.

And then, sure enough, the next day, it was just the same.

George. Good Mews. Just that.

Rigatoni had a few nibbles but then he went outside through the flap to have a think about what was happening.

A great big think.

Rigatoni watched the squirrel.

He scampered about, finding bits and pieces, sitting up on his back legs,

having a munch,

chirruping and leaping along the fence,

onto the old garage,

up a tree and down again.

It gave Rigatoni an idea.

I don't have to stay here waiting for George and Good Mews, do I? I could go out and look for pasta. I can walk and run. I can scamper. I can walk along fences, leap up on to a garage roof and climb a tree. I can do all that. Surely I could go and find someone who will give me some pasta.

This idea felt like a lovely idea. Rigatoni smiled to himself as he thought it. He saw himself arriving at someone's house, singing his "Pastaaaaaaaaa" song and that person coming out and dishing him up a great big bowlful.

Rigatoni let himself have this lovely dream for as long as he could until he shook himself and made himself think quite clearly: *No one is giving me pasta right now, and won't until I go out there and look for it.*

Right now.

Chapter Six

Saying "Right now" to himself gave Rigatoni a push, a bit of drive to get himself to go out there and hunt for pasta!

So Rigatoni climbed a fence,

galloped across the garage roof

and clawed his way carefully down another fence into the garden of the Powell family.

Rigatoni had been there once before. It was when he was out and about exploring.

Rigatoni strolled up to the back door and meowed.

Nothing.

He meowed again.

The door opened and, Heidi, the youngest Powell, came out to see what was going on.

"Oh, look," Heidi called back into the house, "it's the cat from over the back."

Heidi's dad came out and looked.

"Oh yes," he said, "I know that one. I think it's Rigatoni."

"He's hungry," said Heidi.

"Oh yes," said Dad, "cats are always hungry. Or they're asleep. That's about it."

"Have we got any food for him?"

"Oh no," Dad said, "we shouldn't feed him. The thing is, if you feed a cat that isn't yours, it's like stealing a cat from someone else."

"Come on, Dad, you can see he's hungry. We must have some bits to give him."

"No, love," said Dad, "we really shouldn't."

"A little bit of cheese?" Heidi said with her best pleading voice.

"A little bit of cheeeeeeese?"

"Oh all right," Dad said, giving in.

He went indoors and came out again with a bit of cheese on a plate. He gave it to Heidi to give to Rigatoni.

Heidi put it down in front of Rigatoni.

Cheese? he thought. *Cheese? What's the point of cheese without pasta? I didn't come here for cheese.*

He stared at it. Looked back at Dad. Looked at Heidi. Surely they would know that he was a pasta cat. He loved pasta. All he wanted was a bit of pasta. That was easy, wasn't it?

Heidi and Dad looked at him.

They couldn't understand what Rigatoni wanted.

"Well, that's an odd one," said Dad, "first cat I've ever seen that doesn't fancy a bit of cheese. Oh well, perhaps he's not hungry after all."

Rigatoni looked at them and let out the biggest, longest pasta shout that he could:

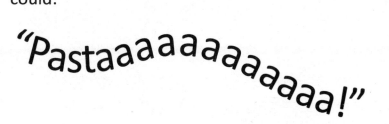

"Pastaaaaaaaaaaaaa!"

Heidi thought he was saying that so that he could get a stroke, so she bent down and stroked Rigatoni.

Nice, thought Rigatoni, *but it's not pasta, is it?*

He stayed for a little bit longer, gave the bit of cheese a quick lick and then turned round, walking off across the garden to find someone else. Someone else who would "get it", that all he wanted was a bowlful of pasta.

Chapter Seven

Rigatoni put his nose in the air and was sure that he could smell pasta. Wasn't it coming from a house a few doors down? He could smell the steamy floury smell of pasta boiling in a pan. He pricked his ears up. He could hear the sound of water bubbling in the pan and a lovely picture came into Rigatoni's head, of Ruth tipping pasta out of the saucepan, straining it so that all the hot water went into the sink — and best bit of all — forking it into Rigatoni's bowl.

Just thinking of that made Rigatoni's belly grumble.

I'll follow the smell and sound of pasta boiling, he said to himself and was soon pushing through a gap in a hedge, up over a fence and then into a backyard.

Yes! This was a house that was cooking pasta!

He stood outside and let out his great pasta cry:

"Pastaaaaaaaa!"

Sure enough, out came someone. It was Antonio. His grandparents came from Italy and Antonio often went to stay with them.

Antonio hadn't met Rigatoni before but he liked the way this strange cat was standing outside his grandparents' house, miaowing so loudly. He laughed.

He shouted back into the house.

Rigatoni could almost see the pasta pot boiling away.

Come on! he thought. *All you've got to do, little chap, is ask someone to give me some?*

But no, Antonio and his grandparents were very kind, and brought him some little bits of ham.

"There, little chap," said Antonio, "something for you to chew, eh?"

Yes, thought Rigatoni, *it is* something *for me to chew, but actually what I'd like much, much, much *more is some of your pasta.*

But they didn't understand.

Instead, while Rigatoni chewed the ham, Antonio and his grandparents came out and sat underneath a canopy to eat their pasta.

This isn't how it's supposed to be, thought Rigatoni. *I should be eating pasta too. If Ruth and Tina were here, they would know. They would each have a bowl and I would have a bowl too!*

Yes, Antonio and the grandparents munched their pasta and looked down kindly at Rigatoni, who gave the ham a bit of a go.

But again,

it was so disappointing.
So dull.
So sad.

How will I get pasta ever again?
Rigatoni thought.

He was beginning to panic now.

George wouldn't give him pasta.

The Powells wouldn't give him pasta.

And now Antonio and his grandparents were not giving him pasta.

It's all hopeless. What can I do?

Chapter Eight

What Rigatoni didn't know was that Antonio's grandparents ran a café. They had just picked up Antonio from his mum, and they were having a snack before heading off to their café. It was called "Paolo and Pietà's Pasta Place". It wasn't far, just a few doors down from their house.

Rigatoni watched them all finishing their pasta. Well, nearly. In fact Antonio's was a bit too much. He couldn't finish his. Rigatoni watched with horror as Antonio got up, went indoors and tipped the last few bits of his fusilli and pesto into the rubbish bin.

What?!

He was tipping it *away*?

Couldn't they see that he was Rigatoni the pasta cat? Couldn't they see that he loved pasta? Couldn't Antonio have just passed his bowl over to him instead of tipping it away? How awful was that?!

Rigatoni had never felt so bad, ever before.

But now that he had seen that this was a family that loved pasta, he thought that it might be worth hanging around with them.

This meant that when Antonio's grandparents locked up, walked across the yard and went out through the back gate with Antonio, Rigatoni followed after them.

"Look," said Antonio, laughing at the sheer fun of it, "the cat is following us."

The grandparents laughed too, pleased to see Antonio so happy.

And yes, Rigatoni followed Antonio and his grandparents along the back street that ran behind the shops and in through the back gate to the café.

"Look," said Antonio, "the cat's come to the café."

Rigatoni took a long, careful look at this place. He had never been here before. He sat on his haunches and waited to see what might turn up.

Antonio brought
out a bit of string
and waved it about
for Rigatoni to
play with.

This is fun,
Rigatoni thought.

He chased it,
nearly caught it,
then did catch it,
then let go of it,
chased it again.
Antonio laughed
and laughed.

After some banging and clanging in the café, Rigatoni heard something very exciting. It was the sound of pasta boiling in a pot. He could smell it too: that lovely hot floury smell.

I wonder what kind of pasta it is, he thought.

Fusilli?

Spaghetti?

Penne?

Linguini?

Tortellini?

Farfalle?

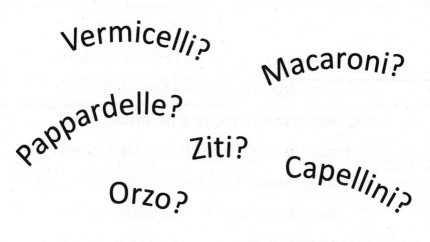

Vermicelli?
Macaroni?
Pappardelle?
Ziti?
Capellini?
Orzo?
Ravioli?
Tagliatelle?

His nose quivered. His ears pricked up at the sound of the bubbles bubbling round the pasta as it got softer and softer. Out came Rigatoni's pasta cry:

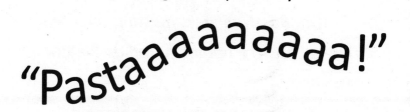

"Pastaaaaaaaa!"

It made Antonio laugh again.

But it seemed to have also made him think something. Some little clue from the way Rigatoni made that noise. What if this cat would like some pasta? It was just a fun thought he had.

So he said to his "nonna" – that's "grandma" in Italian – "Can I give the cat some pasta?"

I think Antonio is getting the right idea! Rigatoni thought.

"You can," said Nonna, "but don't expect him to eat it, Antonio. Cats like meat."

Oh no, Nonna is putting him off. Oh please try again, Antonio! Rigatoni thought.

"Can I try though?" Antonio said.

"Yes, you can," Nonna said and

she poured out some fusilli into a little bowl and gave it to Antonio to give to Rigatoni.

Antonio loved doing this.

"Here you are, little cat," said Antonio, "try this!"

Rigatoni could hardly believe what was going on. How wonderful was this? Finally, someone had realised that the one thing he wanted more than anything else in the world was just this: a bowl of pasta!

Rigatoni pushed his face into the bowl, burying his whiskers in amongst the whirly fusilli, munching and chewing as if he had never eaten anything like it ever before.

It was soooooo lovely. It was so gorgeous to feel the soft, chewy pasta on his tongue and in his cheeks. Whirly, twisty fusilli. Mmmmmm.

"He loves it!" Antonio called out.

"He does!" Nonna said, who was really surprised.

Mmmmmm

"Can we give him some more?"

"I suppose so," Nonna said, "but remember, Antonio, the cat doesn't belong to us. I'm not sure but I think he belongs to that couple who live in one of the flats at the end of the road. I'll go round and tell them about him in a while."

Chapter Nine

Later, Nonna and Antonio went out, leaving Antonio's granddad in charge of the café.

Rigatoni was worried that Nonna and Antonio were going away, just as Ruth and Tina went away, so he quickly made up his mind to follow them.

Where were they going?

Then after just a few steps, he realised that they were heading for his own home. *What's going on?* he wondered. *I hope they don't give me back to George and Good Mews for ever more.*

Outside his home, Nonna rang the doorbell.

But no one came out. Nobody was there. She bent down and peeped through the letter box.

She called out.

"Hello!"

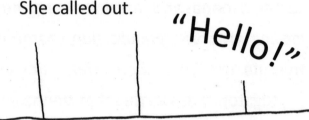

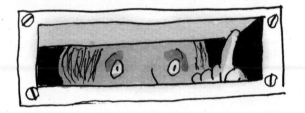

Rigatoni and Antonio stood and waited.

I so hope that they don't make me go back, Rigatoni thought. And then he thought some more: *Well, if they do take me back, I'll just do what I did before, slip out through the cat flap, out the back, up the fence along that garden, over that garage roof, through the gap in the hedge, up that other fence and back at the pasta house. Or I could find my way to the pasta café. I know my way around . . .*

Just then, who should turn up, but George.

He looked at Nonna and Antonio, and down to Rigatoni.

"Oh, he's with you, is he?" he said in a grumpy sort of a way.

"Yes," said Antonio with an excited voice.

"Well, I'm supposed to be looking after him," George said. "I was getting worried that he had run away and something had happened to him," he added.

"No, he's fine," said Nonna, "but if he belongs to you . . ."

"He doesn't belong to me," said George, "it's just my job for a few days." And as he said that, he took another tin of Good Mews out of his pocket.

Rigatoni looked at it as if it was the most dangerous, disgusting thing in the world. How could George think that this was something that *he*, Rigatoni the pasta cat, would like to eat?

He turned away, repelled by the sight of it, his mouth still tasting the lovely fusilli he had been eating earlier.

He heard George and Nonna say a few more things but he wasn't quite sure what, and then Nonna said, "You can tell them, then?"

"Sure," George said and off he went.

He's going! thought Rigatoni. *Without giving me that Good Mews stuff!*

And then Antonio and Nonna walked back to Paolo and Pietà's Pasta Place and Rigatoni followed after them.

Chapter Ten

Another day and a night went by, with Rigatoni spending some time at the café, and some time with Antonio at his grandparents' house.

Sometimes in this time, Rigatoni went out the back to watch the squirrels. He thought how good it was that a squirrel had given him the idea to explore and find his way to a place with pasta.

Sometimes in this time, he lay down in a sunny spot and had a sleep. It helped the pasta go down.

But best of all – not just sometimes, but *several* times – Nonna and Antonio gave Rigatoni some pasta.

Then, the next day Nonna and Antonio readied themselves to go out and Nonna told Antonio to bring his string along to get Rigatoni to follow them.

And he did.

They walked down the street to Rigatoni's home, rang the doorbell and waited.

Oh no, Rigatoni thought. *They've changed their mind. They are taking me back to George and Good Mews. I'll be stuck there for ever more!*

Antonio went on flicking the string and Rigatoni was distracted by it, trying to chase it and catch it.

But no one came to the door.

"That's funny," Nonna said, "I thought that boy said—"

But she didn't finish what she was saying because at that very moment, a car drew up next to them. It was Ruth and Tina!

They had come back.

They hadn't gone away for ever.
They were back!

How exciting was that! Home was back to being as it always was:

Pasta at home.

His favourite place on the cushion on the sofa.

His owners sitting beside him, giving him tickles and strokes: the best feeling in the world.

Everything would be perfect once again.

Antonio, Nonna, Ruth and Tina chatted away on the doorstep, pointing at Rigatoni and laughing. Antonio did an "impression" of Rigatoni eating pasta – munch, munch, munch, with his face in an imaginary bowl – and everyone laughed again.

Ruth and Tina opened the door, went back to get the suitcases and bags, then said goodbye to Antonio and Nonna.

"Thank you so much," Tina said, "and so clever of you to realise that Rigatoni is a pasta cat."

"I thought that he would like Good Mews for a change," Ruth admitted.

"Well, I'm sure George did his best, didn't he, Rigatoni?" Tina said, bending down to tickle his head.

Rigatoni purred. He didn't want to get George into trouble. Yes, he had done his best, it was just that . . . just that George never figured out that Rigatoni only loved pasta.

Chapter Eleven

And that *would* be the end of it all: now Ruth and Tina are back home, Rigatoni is happy that he gets his pasta whenever he wants – especially when he calls out. And Rigatoni is happy with his favourite place on the cushion on the sofa and going out the back to watch the squirrels. Oh, yes.

But there is something else.

Every now and then, Rigatoni thinks of Antonio and Nonna, eating their pasta on the terrace and he wanders off, out the back, up the fence, over the garage roof, across the garden, through the gap in the hedge, up and over another fence to find them.

Or sometimes, if it's a bit later, he finds his way to Paolo and Pietà's Pasta Place, and sits on his haunches out the back and cries out,

"Pastaaaaaaaaaa!"

And Antonio or Nonna brings him a bowl of spaghetti or penne or fusilli or linguini or ziti or vermicelli. And sometimes, if he is very lucky, there might be some lasagne or even some cannelloni for him.

And that is all wonderful.

Even so, he always goes home to Ruth and Tina and his special place on the cushion on the sofa, dreaming and dreaming of his next bowl of pasta.